This book belongs to:

_____Bryna_____

My Old Grandma Lucy
by
Victoria Madeline

TO:

GIVING
GRACEFUL
CARING
GENEROUS
DEVOTED
AMAZING
TREASURED

 Victoria

My old grandma Lucy
knit me a scarf,
it choked me so much
it made me barf.

My old grandma Lucy
knit me a hat,
but I didn't like it,
so I gave it to my cat.

My old grandma Lucy
knit me some mittens,
they didn't fit me,
but they fit my kittens.

My old grandma Lucy
knit me a sweater,
but it got all torn up
by the stormy weather.

My old grandma Lucy
knit me a coat,
guess who ate it?
My pet goat.

My old grandma Lucy
knit me a bag,
but all it did
was slouch and sag.

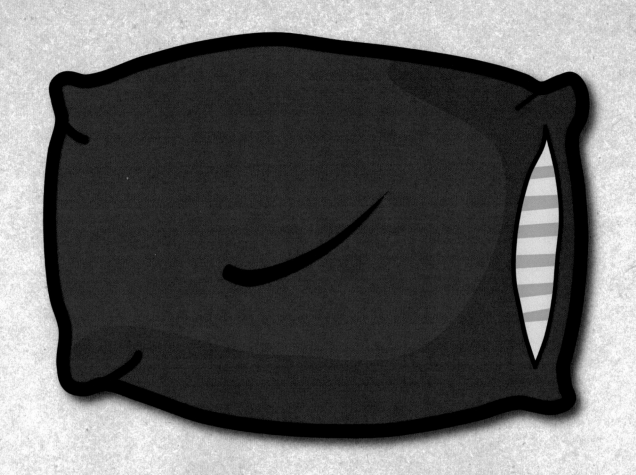

My old grandma Lucy
knit me a pillow,
I just gave it
to my friend Willow.

My old grandma Lucy
knit me a vest,
it scratched my skin
like an itchy pest.

My old grandma Lucy
knit me some socks,
but I just hid them
under some rocks.

My old grandma Lucy
knit me a hoodie,
but I gave that
to my brother Woody.

My old grandma Lucy
knit me a doll,
but I didn't like it,
not at all.

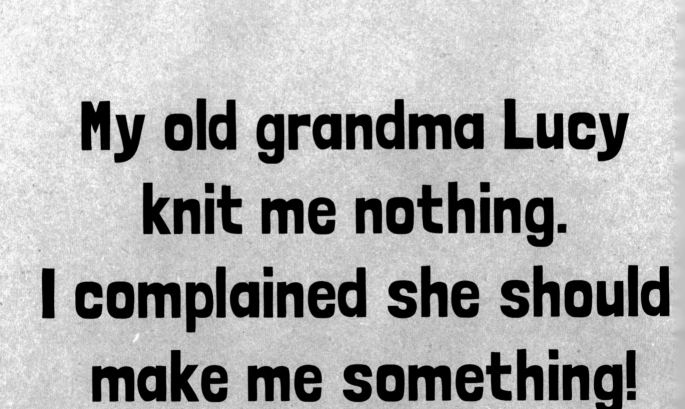

My old grandma Lucy
knit me nothing.
I complained she should
make me something!

My old grandma Lucy
knit me a blanket,
and guess what?
I liked it!

Made in the USA
San Bernardino, CA
01 May 2020